A Man Walks Into A Bar

(and becomes part of the narrative)

Steve Page

Cover Photo by Jez Timms on Unsplash

First Printing: 2022

ISBN: 9798353373346

Imprint: Independently published

What?

Steve's more used to writing poetry but sometimes the words drift off into prose. They may feel like the start of a story, or maybe a scene from a movie that's yet to take form. Some are just curios that raise a smile. Others are imaginings triggered by accounts in the gospels - wondering what happened between the paragraphs.

Who?

Steve is a sometimes poet living in Ealing, London. He's been writing for fun for over 20 years now and more recently has written inspired to write more seriously at Redeemer London, a church for London based in Ealing.

www.redeemerlondon.org

Introduction

These are a mixed bag of stories or the start / part of stories. They were written over several years, some I woke up with, fully framed in my head; others emerged over hours or days.

All gave me great pleasure to write and read aloud. I'm hoping that you'll find pleasure in them too and perhaps be curious as to what happens next, or what happened before, maybe take a shine to a character and imagine a new branch of their story.

Pick up a pen or take up your keyboard and give it a go.

Foreword

I sit face to face, the stage set

For stories to fill the space

I'm free to meander through my head

As the voice on the page leaves little unsaid

It reveals the reflection of a new me

That I so dearly want to be

Seeing what was once misread

Form part of a longer, golden thread

The voice on the page lifts me free

And I find myself in every word he said

Ready for a fresh first person

In my very own new narrative

Bible Prose

The Big Guy

The bar was busy – far busier than usual. Most of the non-regulars were here to see the Big Guy. Word gets around quick round here; we're a small town and mine was only one of two bars open this late.

'The Big Guy' – I call him that cos that's what most people called him when they asked if he really was here, though those who seemed to know him better called him 'Teach'.

"Have you got the Big Guy back there?" "Is Teach here?"

We'd all heard what had happened earlier – most of us new Philip (the bloke who went through the roof and came out walking) and there he was sitting with the Big Guy, celebrating. They sat at the back, at one of the bigger tables, a circular one that gave the Big Guy's stature more of a welcoming presence. It was stacked with plates, bottles and glasses. He'd said to keep them coming and was offering all who could reach in to help themselves, but a lot of the crowd hung back, happy to just take in the spectacle and to get a glance at Phil and the Big Guy together. Something to tell the kids.

We'd stopped the music earlier on account of the singing and laughter. No one was listening to the back track, I don't think they could have even if they'd wanted to, not with his fierce laughter and ebullient voice – and especially when the crowd joined in. His entourage clearly knew the words and the chorus was easy enough to pick up – I swear the rafters were shaking with the storm of his song.

And when he wasn't singing, he was telling stories – drawing laughter and questions in equal measure. I heard something about a sheep and a gold coin, and later lamps and a feast. He seemed to have a bottomless well of story and lessons.

It was refreshing to have a good-natured crowd without the usual discord and violence that comes with wine and late nights. Something about his presence fostered a healthy 'we're-all-family-here' atmosphere.

And we took him at his word, we kept them coming – wine and ale and meat and bread - and I saw what looked like half our stock pass over the bar. Strange thing, but later Rachel said the cellar looked just as full as when we opened earlier, if not more so.

We (Pete, Rachel and me) did our best to keep up with the orders but at around 11 I sent my son out to go fetch Jonny and Ben. I'd have to pay them time and a half, but I knew we'd not be able to keep up for much longer. He smiled and said they were already here and were in the kitchen.

At 2 am it felt like half the town was here and I started getting worried about the local ordinances, but I needn't have worried – those town enforcement officers that we had were here too, each enjoying the party, and I think I saw most of the town council drinking and eating and singing along.

At 4 am I summoned the courage to ask him – I needed to ask, was he planning on staying much longer?

Strange thing – once I got close, I saw that he wasn't that big. He seemed just a regular sized guy and looking at him I wondered why he had such a presence. Then he looked at me and smiled and he seemed to fill the room.

He kept on smiling as I spoke and then he said something about him not being here that often, and we should make the most of it. And that look of his, with his hand on my shoulder, told me it would be okay, and I should settle in for a long day. The Big Guy was going to make his short stay something to be remembered for a long while. Capernaum was going to be talking about this for years to come.

[An imagining based on the account in the gospel of Mark, chapter 2.]

First Stone

Look at her! She doesn't deserve to live! The law is clear. Death by stoning. We have a God-given responsibility. Anything less than the swift application of the full weight of the law will send the wrong message to our young people. The word will go out that our community condones this filthy behaviour. If she gets away with this it will give the green light to every woman who wants to undermine the sanctity of marriage.

Stone her! Let's get it done, before she can infect anyone else with her promiscuous behaviour.

No! Don't even think about that. Don't waste time trying to use this to entrap the country teacher – yes it would put him is a tough spot and show him up as the fraud that he is, but we mustn't delay. Every minute she's still breathing brings shame on her family and her community – for all our sakes, let's just get this done.

Okay – I can see it would put the country preacher in a difficult position, but I can't believe you would want to make political capital out of this – it's a simple local matter that should be dealt with swiftly and decisively.

Okay, okay. I see that. But we must get this done today.

[Can't believe I'm agreeing to this – what would Moses say?]

3 The teachers of the law and the Pharisees brought in a woman caught in adultery. They made her stand before the group 4 and said to Jesus, "Teacher, this woman was caught in the act of adultery. 5 In the Law Moses commanded us to stone such women. Now what do you say?" 6 They were using this question as a trap, in order to have a basis for accusing him. But Jesus bent down and started to write on the ground with his finger.

>>>John 8: 3 - 6<<<

Can you believe this guy? What's he thinking? Has he got nothing to say about this? It's a simple enough question. And look at her – she just can't help herself, standing there weeping, trying the come-on, as if SHE is the victim here. I see what's she's doing. Making me, making us, want her. Giving us ideas. She has no shame. Why are we waiting? What's he gonna say that will change anything?

What's that? What's he saying?

7 When they kept on questioning him, he straightened up and said to them, "Let any one of you who is without sin be the first to throw a stone at her." 8 Again he stooped down and wrote on the ground.

>>>John 8: 7-8<<<

--What? Without sin? Is that a new thing? - Now we need to be innocent to carry out God's just punishment? Is this some kinda joke?

No, don't listen to him – he's just time-wasting – he's let her get to him! We need to do this now! Don't look at me like that. Dad, what are you doing? Don't... you'll need that rock in a moment. Pick it up! Don't walk away! Oh, come on! Jude, no. not you too. Zeb, come back – what's wrong with you?

Well, if you've not got the stomach for this, I have! What's wrong with you people! Oh, no – don't look at me like that; you're no more than a halfwit from the countryside. You have no idea what we face every day from these prostitutes. I know what you're thinking, but at least I have the mettle to hold these rocks – I know what's right!

Okay – so I skim a little off the top every now and then. That doesn't mean I can't recognise a harlot when I see one.

Okay, yes, alright – my eyes might linger longer than they should sometimes. But that's because of the way they dress – it's indecent, that's what it is. Our children shouldn't be exposed to that.

Okay – so I'm not completely truthful in my dealings with customers – but that's just salesmanship, everyone does it – I need to stay competitive. I can still deal out justice for my community.

And yes, alright, I'm a little imaginative with my accounting, but the taxes are so scandalously high.

Yes. I curse. My language can get a little coarse once in a while – but that's just guy talk. You're looking at me as if I'm the sinful one.

Okay – yes – I get angry. And yes, I say stuff I regret. But no more than the next guy.

Oh. Yeah. I'm not proud of that time with Miriam. But she got me drunk. I'm not normally like that.

No – I'm not proud of that.

Yeah, I'd forgotten about that as well.

Oh. Yeah, I regret that day too. Man, these rocks are heavy. Where is everyone?

Oh, hell! Okay, okay – you might be right, perhaps I don't quality to make accusations, but what she did was wrong – it's the law! And the full weight of the -

... Oh hell. Yeah, I get it. Fine! I'm going. But this isn't fair! You know it's not fair! It's unjustified! It's undeserved mercy! What is this world coming to.

9 At this, those who heard began to go away one at a time, the older ones first, until only Jesus was left, with the woman still standing there. 10 Jesus straightened up and asked her, "Woman, where are they? Has no one condemned you?" 11 "No one, sir," she said. "Then neither do I condemn you," Jesus declared. "Go now and leave your life of sin."

>>>John 8: 10-11<<<

Playing at being Jesus

Mr Parsons had made it sound exciting, but mum told Joan that she was wicked. She wasn't allowed her dolls for a week, a week she spent bemused and resentful, and she refused to poo for three days until mum relented and gave her Barbie back – but the rest would have to wait.

It had begun with Mr Parsons at Sunday School with his story of the blind man and the mud and the spit.* We'd sat on the adult chairs in a circle: me, Joan, Gemma, Charlie, and the Brown sisters, knee to knee in a circle in the corner of the hall, the one with the draft and the stacked chairs reminding us that we were the remnant of a once thriving community.

He told us how Jesus made a paste of mud and spit [Charlie thought this hilarious and spat at Gemma, so he had to stand with his nose on the wall for the rest of the lesson] and how Jesus slathered it on the man's eyes and then told him (unnecessarily we thought) to go wash it off. It hadn't worked first time – was that a first for Jesus? we speculated and the second time the bloke saw people again, but he was told to keep it secret, which made no sense.

So that afternoon, after dinner, Joan got mud from the garden, and pasted it onto barbie's legs which were abnormally long and made her topple over and on my action man's face on account of his facial scar which I thought looked cool, but was curious to see what happened. She pasted it on Ken and Sindy too, but not for any specific ailment. She followed the prescribed method, slather, wash and then repeat (which I think she enjoyed a little too much to be honest) but after the second wash there was no sign of any healing, perhaps because, like mum said, she was so wicked, unlike Jesus of course.

I'd never seen mum go that colour – she was livid.

She told Joan to go wash the mud stains off her hands and to put her dress in the wash. Joan couldn't be Jesus and it was wrong to think she could. That sort of thing wasn't for little girls.

The next Sunday Mr Parsons seemed a little miffed. He and dad and mum sat in the hall, knee to knee, for ages. I thought we were for the high jump, but afterwards mum looked like a naughty child. She was very quiet and at dinner dad said that she had something to say - to our horror, she apologised in front of all of us and she told Joan it was okay to try and do what Jesus did. It was what he would have wanted.

We were so ashamed for my mum - neither of us tried to be Jesus ever again.

**Found in the gospel of John, chapter 9.*

The Right Nail

Settle down please. Today you will be trained in Level 1 crucifixion good practice.

First, the nail. Please pass the bag along once you have taken one nail each. You can rely on these nails. Each one is forged by hand, hammered out and shaped with skill. 'You can nail it with one nail,' as they say.

Nails can be used to fasten almost anything to wood. Choosing the right nail for the job can make a big difference in hold power. As there is no need to conceal the nail head and we require maximum holding power, we have chosen common nails for the job. When the nail is temporary and will be pulled out again, as with crucifixion work, we have found that a double-headed or duplex nail is the best choice.

Experience and common practice calls for driving the nail through the thinner limb into the thicker timber. For maximum holding power, the length of the nail is such that it passes almost, but not quite, through the thicker timber. For best results, lay the condemned on the crossbeam and bind the arms in place on the timber before nailing. I refer you to your ropes and knots training last week.

One nail is sufficient for each limb if placed between the forearm bones above the wrist. You will find that some limbs will have been subject to a break beforehand. If this is the case, we advise that you use additional rope to bind the limb to the cross beam and that you select a site for the nail further up the arm if necessary.

Before lifting the cruciform into the hollow, ensure each nail has been driven in securely. Once you and your supervisor is satisfied, lift the cruciform in one swift movement ensuring the base slides neatly into the hollow.

This is the greatest test for your handiwork.

The impact of the timber landing at the base of the hollow will cause the body to jar under its own weight and place downward pressure on the nail. If a nail comes lose, you are advised to lift the cruciform out of its hollow, lay it down and use a second nail on the unsecured limb.

In most cases this will not be necessary, and the condemned will hang securely long enough to allow the body to die, even if this takes several days. Once death has been confirmed using the accepted method, lift the cruciform down, remove the nails and inspect them for damage. If deemed reusable, rinse and dry them before storage.

If there are no questions you will now each be assigned to an experienced colleague to assist with a crucifixion. If at any time you feel that you are likely to vomit, please use the bucket provided. There's no shame in this, the first time can be quite shocking, but you will soon learn how to complete the exercise with professionalism. Please keep your nail, you'll need it later.

[An imagining triggered by the account of the crucifixion of Jesus in the gospel of John, chapter 19.]

A man walks into a bar ...

A man walks into a bar. It's quiet. He sees his friend sitting on a stool, halfway along the bar, nursing a glass of red wine - untouched by the look of it.

Weird, thinks the man, seeing him alone, his friend usually has company. Where's the rest of them?

"Hi."

"Hi. Where have you been?"

"What do you mean?"

"I've been waiting."

"Oh, - right." Then the man remembers.

"Sorry – been a little distracted."

His friend doesn't answer. He just looks into his glass, like he's not sure why he ordered it. And then he looks up at the man, like he knows it's not his turn to speak yet.

The man says, "I've been distracted," then he remembers he's said that already.

His friend smiles and gives a half nod and the man fills the silence with a tear or two as the truth sinks in.

The man takes a breath and says, "Can I have a drink?"

Another half nod, this time to the woman behind the bar the man hasn't noticed and he feels guilty at that, but isn't sure why. Then he sees her name badge, Sophia, and he knows that means something. She pours him a tall soda and lime - lots of ice. And the man wonders how she knew. Then he looks at her name again and swallows his question. She knows stuff. He hopes, with a little guilt, that she's the silent type, he's not sure he can stomach any more right now, he's still swallowing his friend's unspoken questions – and they were always sure to serve up truths, no matter how unpalatable they might be.

"Can we sit in a booth?"

"Good idea."

They sit and Sophia brings over a menu, but the man lays it flat rather than look at what's on offer.

His friend still has his glass and still leaves it untouched, which gives the man a shiver of remembrance. But his friend looks at ease and sits back, ready for the wait for the man to get uncomfortable enough to speak.

It doesn't take long.

Starting with excuses, then the blame, followed by the regret – it's not long before the man gets to the place where he finds the words he's been looking for – "I'm sor - "

Before he can get the last syllable out his sob takes over

The man can't look at his friend now and closes his eyes tight, holding then closed with his thumb and forefinger – pushing the hurt back, trying to get to the next corner. Then he feels his friend's hand cover his hand on the table and rest there. And with a small shudder the man becomes aware of the contours of his friend's scars and he turns his hand over and they grasp one another. The man breaths in deep, grateful for his friend's strong grip.

"I'm – sorry." The man still doesn't open his eyes.

"Yes?"

"I'm sorry. I walked out on you. I ran. I abandoned you. ... I took the easy way out."

His friend's hold gets a little stronger at that. Still the man doesn't look up. And then his worst nightmare –

"Peter, do you love me?"

His head jerks up – straight into the path of those eyes that see everything.

"Lord, you know I do." Please believe me, the man shouts inside as he grips all the harder.

"Do you?"

The man squeezes his eye shut again, unable to take the weight of that gaze. Then he braces, lifts his head and takes the full force of that look. "Lord, you know I love you."

"But, do you?"

The man can feel the sob coming again, but fights it down. "Yes, I love you."

And with that last confession, the man feels the denial fall off his chest, from his arms, from his leaden legs and his tears find release. And after a moment, they laugh and his friend pulls him in for a long embrace over the table and as the man wipes his face and takes a swallow of his soda and lime, Jesus picks up the menu and orders the fish.

And as the food arrives so do his other friends and they pull over more tables and stay in the bar all day, with so much to say to one another, until eventually Sophia comes over to interrupt the laughter and says, "don't you have homes to go to?"

And they all laugh again – and Peter's laugh is the loudest, happy with the truth, that they are home.

[An imagining based on the account in the gospel of John, chapter 21.]

Messy Church

'Acts 6:1

"In those days when the number of disciples was increasing, the Hellenistic [Greek Speaking] Jews among them complained against the Hebraic Jews because their widows were being overlooked in the daily distribution of food…."

And in the next church office staff meeting (which wasn't until Tuesday, because Martha was away on a training course on the Monday), the distribution of food was raised as part of the staff meeting agenda.

Levi welcomed Martha back and said the office had not been the same without her.

On the topic of food distribution, Joseph noted for the minutes that he was aware of the improper completion of the application form for the distribution for food and he had set an email out to the church 3 weeks previously with an easy-to-follow guide to help those less familiar with excel.

Mary suggested that the email be sent out again as a reminder in case people had not yet managed to read it, because she for one couldn't remember receiving it.

Martha noted that the amount of food donated was increasing each week, and that the weekly notices should include a note of thanks for the church members' generosity. Everyone agreed and Levi asked that the minutes also note the church's thanks to Martha for spearheading the project.

Martha said that the food distribution project had been running for several months now and that she had handed the day-to-day project management over to Benjamin, the new intern, who really appreciated the opportunity to take on more responsibility and was very keen to make a success of it. Levi reminded everyone of their earlier discussion about delegating more and said this was a really good example of trusting others to get on with the job.

Timothy suggested that perhaps there was a more fundamental issue that needed to be addressed about how well the Greek speaking Jews were being integrated into the church, for example whether they were benefiting proportionality from the food distribution. Levi said that he would take that discussion offline as it was slightly off topic.

Philip said he agreed with Timothy and that perhaps it was worth exploring here while the team was together.

Levi acknowledged the issue but said that perhaps Timothy, Philip and he speak privately about it.

Martha said that she was sure Timothy and Phillip weren't implying that there was any bias in the way food was being distributed. She went on to set out how many of her friends were Greek speaking and her own daughter had been named Nicola – so no one could accuse her of not embracing the multi-ethnic nature of the new church.

Levi said that he was sure there was no suggestion of bias.

Martha said she would like to hear this from Timothy and Philip, because it had certainly been implied.

Levi suggested they take a break and come back at 11.

Martha said she needed some air and would step out for a few minutes. Mary went with her.

[ ]

After the break Timothy said he wanted to place on record that he was very grateful for the hard work Martha had put into the setting up of the food distribution and said that he in no way thought she had overseen an unfair distribution of food. Phillip said he echoed this.

Martha thanked them for putting the record straight and suggested that if there had been individuals who felt that they had been overlooked, Benjamin would speak to them individually.

Levi said the next item on the agenda was the staff picnic.

Transcription

He’s talking faster now like he knows his time is shorter than before. He flies from the Law to fresh words of grace and I struggle to keep pace with his passion that threatens to overwhelm his frail, well-travelled frame. Words that inspire, even as they are inspired, fired thick and fast, finding their target, embedded in my inscription as I seek the gift of accurate Word-made-flesh-made-word on paper transcription.

And now as I sit with fingers quivering, taking time out while I can while he's sleeping, I pray that the inspiration for the words that he's speaking will be equalled by my quick ears and matched by my quicker scrawling so that the church will hear just what the Lord is saying and they can read the truth that is theirs for the believing.

I wonder if transcription is a spiritual gift?

[Triggered by Romans 16:22

"I, Tertius, who wrote down this letter, greet you in the Lord."]

Everyday Prose

Southbank 11 am

As I wait, I see her on an uncomfortably high stool - the grandmother perching opposite the comfortably bored teenager, replete in his distressed Ramones tee shirt and ripped white jeans.

She holds her black coffee still with both hands, while he plays with the long spoon in his tall glass of hot chocolate, her eyes focused on the top of his head, his engrossed in the puddle of brown milk around his saucer. Below the music, she pleads for a relationship that he shows no interest in until she reaches into her bag and emerges with perhaps something that he's been waiting for –

And beyond the counter, shielded by formica, percolators and stacked cups, the apprentice barista drops his tray and from the back two men in ill-fitting suits give a half-hearted cheer, while his boss withholds her anger in front of the paying customers, but judging by her face she would gladly take her protégé by his stained apron and string him up. I think this isn't the first time she's taken the cost of breakages out of his salary.

And I've missed what it is grandma has presented to her grandson – all I can see is a suggestion of his fingers playing with silver, a ring perhaps? The hot chocolate is pushed aside, and his shoulders straighten. She still looks uncertain, and the seconds drag until his face seems to soften. He looks up and mouths what might be a 'thank you'.

And he doesn't withdraw his hand when she covers it with her own.

The third and last date

The pub is busy, but he sits quietly while she explains patiently what it is he really wants if only he'd pay heed and listen and not have the stress of second guessing himself. And in his quiet, in the soft breeze of her advice, he runs through past perfectly good menu options and considers how their taste agreed with him.

He resolves and waits and before dessert he explains he needs to leave and walk the dog. And once home, old Pippa loves him for who he is and he gratefully takes the lead, while blocking one more number on his Nokia.

Gran the hero

My return was announced with a half-felt, tannoid, 'London'. But in the automated female voice it sounded more like 'Long Gone'. Maybe it knew something I didn't.

I'd always considered London to be a city which gave you permission to be yourself, but right now I doubted who that was. The press might decide for me or I'd be left with a choice: establish a me that incorporated my lesser known family history or try to continue living the me I'd firmly established before today's funeral.

Did I have time to make my own decision? Or would tomorrow's red tops take the initiative? I had ignored my agent's repeated calls on the journey back. I wasn't sure what to tell her. Whatever slant tomorrow's headlines would take, today I needed a drink.

I met Toby at the Red Lion - a long established home-from-home close to the studios.

Thanks to WhatsApp he'd seen me coming and had bought me a dark cider and found a dark corner table. It was typical of him to anticipate my need for a quiet space and the opportunity to talk if I wanted it.

'Drink,' he said firmly. I sat and we sat in silence while I supped my cider halfway down the glass. Toby simply smiled and worked his way through his over ladened fish finger sandwich and a soda and lime.

I took a breath and cracked the silence while he started the other half of his sandwich. 'It wasn't the grand affair that I expected, but Gran had a decent send off.' Toby nodded, tartar sauce staining his chin.

'Mum was her normal withdrawn self and Sis took charge.

'Gran's chums were out in force in their blazers and the home office sent a soul representative. I thought they'd long forgotten her, but no. Reuters was there too.'

Toby nodded with a full mouth. He'd never met my family, but knew them well enough from my stories and occasional rant. He knew the presence of the press wasn't unexpected, with or without me there.

I thought about telling him about what I had in my bag, but it could wait.

'The service was at the local parish church. The vicar either knew her well or faked it like a pro. At least he told the full story without embellishment.'

Gran had retired to Woolton-on-the-Marsh and had spent the best part of 25 years as part of their community while still maintaining her old network.

'He was brief and to the point - just the right amount of sober reflection with a few well-placed anecdotes about the war years. Smiles and tears were there in equal measure.

'Most of the crowd went back to the Royal Legion for refs. Someone, probably Sis, had placed handfuls of old black and whites from Gran's glory days around the tables to reminisce over. And of course, there were plenty of Gran with the great and the good and the not so good.'

Blow it - I might as well tell him. 'And as the eldest grandchild, I was handed custody of her medals.'

Toby stopped mid chew and swallowed the bread down, 'What - even the ...?'

'Yes'

'Blimey, do you have them here?'

'Yes'

'What will you do with the - you know...?'

'Keep it I think - it is part of the family history. It's history.'

'Can I see it?'

I sighed. But I didn't answer. I took another swig of cider and lifted my bag to my lap.

The battered cases were deceivingly light in my hand.

I opened each case and set them on the table, side by side. Neither made any sense. She had no military record as far as we had been able to establish. But there it was - Gran had seen active service and served with honour. It had never been clear to me the exact circumstances of each. She never explained. It was never discussed, but the vicar had included both in his eulogy without explanation - "her proud achievements." I can only assume that Reuters took down every word and that I would soon be linked to the tale.

Toby didn't pick up either medal; like me he simply stared at the odd pair as I mulled this over - probably just as aware as I was of the ramifications for me and my career. We sat in silence until my phoned chirped - a Google news alert -

'ACTION HERO'S FAMILY SHAME'.

I sighed. Not for the first time they had the story wrong. Not shame. I had no doubt of the righteousness of her motives. My Gran did nothing by halves. She threw herself into everything she did and she did it well. Not shame, but a bag full of questions.

We sat and stared at the two medals. How on earth did Gran earn the red ribboned Victoria Cross? And what the hell did she do to earn the silver German Cross?

The bold black swastika stared back at us, offering no explanation.

The bridge character

The bridge character is essential to the narrative, it's just not her narrative.

But later (as if because the readers have asked for more, as if something about her caught their imagination, prompting fresh questions), she may feature again and the panels will frame more detail, more of her back story, her self-motivation and perhaps we will learn her true name.

In a few years' time it may be that a fan develops into a writer, or perhaps an editor, and a story will be commissioned telling her history with colour, with space and we'll see, at last, her scars and at last we'll see the essential essence of how she came to be. And perhaps then we'll identify with her all the more.

One night when we look back when we read again that first appearance, we might realise that there remains some unexplained detail, a few missing pieces of her jigsaw and as we put the final touches to our too tight cosplay costume, we'll wait with hope for her own title that just might reveal her full narrative.

And sometime later we'll message our friends with news that she's being played by your favourite actor in the next summer blockbuster and she's just how we imagined her. But then the movie might well tank and we go back to the refuge of the comic art and stories that first connected with us and resolve to wear that outfit at the next convention lest others write her off along with the movie.

She's more than a bridge character – she really is.

On the door at Fashion Week at Uni

They were a common-or-garden, run-of-the-mill variety of right-weird bleeders.

Individually nothing I'd not seen before, but oh boy, together - it was like the circus had passed through and their apprentice scheme had got left behind. You could see what they were attempting mind you and if we give them a few years I'm sure they will figure out a style and colour scheme that worked.

Then they'll be the envy of us all I expect.

For now... well like I say - right weird bleeders.

Silvi

It was a busy night with room only for small talk around the dark stained table. She sat in half shadow, as still as Bambi after the gunshot and just as alone. And they talked.

At her fingertips her glass brooded, part full of a rich emptiness and part of potential, the combination reeking of a love unexplored with a whiff of harboured regret.

They talked knee to knee and shoulder to shoulder, all smiles and pork scratchings.

She sat and left her past week buried like old sorrow, glad to listen to those with less to say while despair trickled down her left cheek, unnoticed.

They talked, voices lost in the clamour of glasses and the void of wet laughter.

"You're quiet tonight, Silvi. Your Tom not around this week?"

"No, not this week."

She sat and they talked, knee to knee and miles apart.

Smiles of magic

Zero cubed has no more value than zero squared, but is a more pleasant shape and able to bear greater weight. It always reminds me of a spell I learned as a teen from the rag and bone man who was never in a hurry and was always happy to chat, sharing his experience which came from many roads and long hot summers in the '50s when he was younger and less careful.

Zero, he told me, is a useful start to many constructions and worth mastering if you ever intend to move on to primes. Primes are slippery, he explained, and require focus. Zeros similarly require a focused mind, but are easier to build with.

So I spent the summer of '74 getting used to the feel and texture of various zeros, then carefully moved on to zero squared. By the September, just before school, I'd started playing with zeros cubed with not a little success. I picked them up again in the Christmas holidays and then, almost by accident, came across the spell: zero times zero times zero divided by infinity. It still makes me smile.

The following Spring, I discovered girls. And for the next 6 years I put the zeros aside until of course I picked it up at Cambridge, where magic became more generally accepted.

We've learned much since then – and magic has become almost a mainstream discipline. But every now and then, as I stare into the cosmos, I remember that wise old bloke, the summer of 1974 and my first smiles of magic.

Questions with no answers

"I'm going to ask you a series of questions. There's nothing to worry about. You can relax. There's no right or wrong answers, you can..."

"What's the point of that?"

"I'm sorry?"

"What's the point of asking me questions there's no answers to?"

"No. There are answers, just no right or wrong answers."

"I don't think there's any other kind."

"What do you mean?"

"There's ONLY right or wrong answers. Answers are either right or wrong. Otherwise, what's the point."

"I think you'll get it once we get going. Let's start and we can circle back to this."

"...."

"Really – you'll see. Try this for example: How would you describe the kind of world you'd like your children to grow up in?"

"...is that a trick question?"

"No – it's an honest question – How would you describe –

"Wait – what? How can you have an honest question? Answers can be honest or dishonest – questions are just questions. You are way, way messed up. You're wasting my time. Can I have another coke?"

"Yeah, sure – can we have another 2 diet cokes over here? Thank you. Do you want anything to eat?"

"See that is the kind of question that will get a right answer. Yes – ham salad sandwich and chips with mayo."

"That is an honest and right answer – okay. And can we have – oh, you heard that? Okay, and I'll have a hotdog with ketchup and onions. Yeah, I know, but it's my honest answer.

[Both smiled.]

"Can we start again?"

"Yeah, sure."

Can I ask your opinion on a few things?"

"Opinion? Why do you want my opinion?"

"Because it'll be different to mine and I'm curious."

"It might not be."

"Might not be what?"

"Different to yours."

"I guess that's true."

"Let's not go there again – "

"Fair enough – here's what I'd like to ask: Imagine you have a kid –

"How old?"

"[sigh] 9, he's a boy – he looks like your brother and is smarter than you expected and also plays real good football – okay? Imagine – don't matter the details of what he looks like - just imagine you have a kid and so you'd like him to have a good life."

"…"

"You thinking? You feeling what it'll be like to have a kid?"

"Yeah – a bit disconcerting."

"That's right – you got it. Perfect. What kind of world would you like him to grow up in and be a man in and have a kid and raise him in?"

"One with less questions and more answers."

"Tell me more about that."

"... I'd like people to pay more attention – so they don't need to ask dumb questions, we don't have to explain ourselves endlessly, we can just let them be, like, listening and watching and understanding and not asking us to justify and explain – less explaining, more just doing and being together with no upsets and arguments and fights and battles and wars and none of kind of greed that makes you blind to what others need and more of the kind of greed that makes us keen to help. Less shouting. More giving. Less money. More ham sandwiches with chips and mayo. Thank you.

[sound of munching]

"I'd like him to live in a world where you know what you want. You don't, um, you don't have to think too much about it or explain it to yourself or to your mum. And people won't say 'no, you can't have that'. Even when you know that they don't really care one way or another, not really, but they think they need to say no to make you grow up better. I hate that.

"No rules?"

"What? Oh – yes of course they'd be rules, but ones that everyone understands that they need to be there and so keep to them without hating them. Rules. Everyone needs rules – just not different rules for different people. That's dumb. It's what causes wars."

"What kind of wars do rules cause?"

"Nope – don't do that."

"Don't do what?"

"Do ask dumb questions to make me explain myself – just listen and watch and understand - less explaining, I told you."

"Okay. Okay, I'm listening."

"Huh. Well, listen to me." (dip chips in the mayo). "And can you wipe that ketchup off your chin."

[wipe]

"ketchup isn't good. I prefer mayo. The colour is better and thicker."

"okay, I'm listening."

"Ketchup is harder to get rid of. There's too much of it. Mayo comes in little cups and you ask for more when you need it if you have too many chips. Ketchup is always too much and it leaves a mark on your plate and you have to wash it down the drain. And get it off your hands. And off mum's dress. Its not as thick as they pretend. It leaks more. ... Can they take that away? Your plate and tissue. Yeah.

"..."

"Thank you for listening and not talking so much – the men, they talked a lot. Then they stamped and shouted and mum stopped talking....

"When it went dark and I came out there was too much ketchup and it smelt wrong. It tasted wrong. Mum was quiet. [boy begins to cry quietly]

"I'm listening."

"My mum – is she going to be okay?"

"Do you want an honest answer?"

"I want a right answer."

[Scene fades to black]

Family funeral circa 1978

I watched, fascinated, at each Stag standing, legs splayed wide, chest expanding, one hand playing pocket billiards, the other cupping an imperial panetella, or the odd fag-end of a king-sized silk cut. I watched each Cock strutting, squinting against the improbably impressive smoke signals emanating from a side grimace, indicating not just contemplation of past glories, and an absent kin, but a surprising level of self-congratulation and not solo signals, but a tribe-wide cloud of pride, bellowing in resonance, creating a crescendo of 'you just know they would have loved this,' coupled with an elaborate semaphore display that would put any plume of peacocks to shame.

My family gathered to mark their history, to reinforce a crucial coupler of family territory, to shout their quiet authority like ancient royalty, as monarchs of this urban manor, their laughter rising in assumptive victory, leaving no doubt that this clan would face all future threats with no more than 'a quiet word' and a micro-assertion of their claim over their ancestral turf.

I watched my forever-family, my forever-England, planted secure in my ever-after summer, on this once green, scorched earth.

Grandad's leopard-skin leotard

I only have one photo of Grandad from his years of service in the Great War, and in it he's wearing a leopard-skin leotard.

My paternal grandfather, Grandad, was brought up in Brockley, South-East London. In his teens he was conscripted and became a gunner sergeant in the Royal Field Artillery. I still have his stirrups and his French/English phrase book which includes useful words, like dysentery. Think of the movie, 'War Horse', and you're almost there. He fought in the mud in France and put a lot of horses out of their misery.

Apparently, he also enjoyed the stage, a song and a dance, and almost went professional after a string of successful nights at the local Roxy, all of which makes me want to have known him better, but he died in my teens. He laughed a lot, loved his vegetable garden and had a collection of handy-sized, hard-back books giving details of how various circuits and wiring worked. I recall his bear of an armchair and how it was in easy reach of a slim stack of shallow drawers from which he would take slender tools or small curios and sit and explain their significance to my bemused child self.

I have the brown photo somewhere - it's not one I'd like to frame as it raises too many questions for me. Like – is that bloke next to grandad meant to be Robinson Crusoe? Like – what prompted grandad to 'black up' from head to toe – is he Man Friday?

And now, I stare at the photo handed to me by my friend of his grandfather, complete with rifle and medals, and again I silently ask my grandad – why?

Chaplin was French

She could have sworn Charlie Chaplin was French.

She had thought so since childhood - there was something about his movies being sub-titled, his facial hair and (she lowered her voice with some shame) his trouser.

She had loved his films since watching them with her dad and he never had mentioned the silent star's heritage. I mean, why would he?

She looked again. And again, there was something continental in his eye liner, in his gait and in the way that he gracefully pivoted that still fitted her misconception.

But now that she thought more about it, it made perfect sense, of course - he must have been German.

Pharmacy Poetry

"I'll leave you all the weapons for that", Pat smiled and perched the two too-tall cinnamon buns down beside me on the windowsill, as promised fully armed with knife, fork and serviette.

I scaled the bun and caught the eye of the postman as he fought with his cart along the too narrow, not-quite-cobbled path, slick with rain, and then he nodded and gave way to the guy in the slow sports wheelchair while the young mum wrestled her twin girls up past the town hall and gallery, perhaps with the promise of grandma's cookies.

All this while Jill's coffee brewed patiently alongside the buns as she and Deb caught up with long lasting laughter and stories of future ventures.

Welcome to the pharmacy, for poetry.

https://www.thepoetrypharmacy.com/ [A café/bookshop.]

My mother

[after Cynthia Miller's Dropka]

In her previous life, my mother must have been an architect. She brought her vision, her love of precision, her stability to every family occasion - ensuring the family structure was sustainable and capable of longer-term development - and we still bear her signature style.

In her previous life, I'm sure my mother was a portrait painter - able to take a fresh canvas, such as mine and my sisters', and add layer upon layer of colour, of texture, to portray what she saw we would become – each proudly bearing her inscription.

In her previous life, I expect my mother was a pioneer – not of paths yet travelled, but of more frequented avenues, boldly exploring the details and intersections between friends and neighbours helping us rediscover what we had in common - each fresh bond bearing her seal.

In this life, my mother was an endurance athlete, a gifted healer, a 5-star chef, a respected teacher, a talented mediator, a wise counsellor, an innovative financier, a diligent archivist, and our chief story-teller.

In this life, she was my mother.

Dorcis Avenue

I'm at home and I'm making a mug of tea and butter a slice of toast and in a blink there's her smile to the sound of The Express being folded, crossword almost complete, as she rises for a kiss and a 'hello love', and the trusted 'I've got the kettle on'.

We hug and I sit as she stands and takes down two mugs, just as she recalls something or another that she meant to give me last visit and now wonders where she placed for safe keeping for this moment - and she's gone, leaving me sitting in the kitchen resting in the familiarity of her calls from the other room telling me she'll find it in a sec and chiding herself,

- until her cry of finding and her return with something of my dad's that she thought I'd like or perhaps a grey photo, with a young me, head sliced to fit a frame long discarded, but having left its trace with a stain of Sellotape

- and then we talk of nothing but people and happenings that left family stains that we cherish for the pictures they conjure and for the bond left undiminished by time and if anything made stronger by any mug of tea and toast and the still left-unlocked front door always ready to receive me with a 'hello love' from deep within the home that stayed open forever and now keeps a space open for sudden memories.

And back here, now, at home I blink and give a silent undertaking that I'll somehow perpetuate her welcome.

I Spy

One click of a radio button and I'm back in the back of dad's Hillman Minx, to journeys once forgotten, DB5 in my right hand, Lady Penelope's Rolls in the left - both harbouring hidden missiles and secret missions, racing to grandma's baked cherry biscuits deep in darkest green Tonbridge.

Give me the right Junior Choice tune and I'm back, staring at the back of my dad's Brylcreemed hair, breathing in his rationed St. Bruno flakes, while keeping a careful eye on Jenny's wicked swinging skin-breaker buckles.

I'm nose deep in my latest I Spy, ticking off far more than I see, in a race to complete the list before we leave the A23, while nodding to the rhythm of mum's monochrome, high speed knitting.

2 minutes 20 later the song closes and I'm back from my 1960's jaunt, back in my 50's, with part of me still back there, one back seat song from long family car trips, back where I still belong.

River Shuttle

When the tidal wave came I was looking the other way.

I knew the gentle Shuttle had its shallow banks concreted, walled, ready for the diverted torrent, but for some reason I was looking North, thinking that way lay the Thames and its barrier.

I hadn't realised the wave would follow the Shuttle's more meandering route and so I got it in the back of the neck.

The roofer's first visit

I breath in to find my inner Geezer ready to speak with a more common vernacular. I channel my South Londoner and ensure I have my chipped mugs ready out on the counter.

I pull the Nescafe and PG Tips forward from the dusty recesses of the top cupboard and locate the white sugar, checking that I have at least five heaped teaspoons' worth for the coming encounter.

Later, from behind the net curtains, I see him sizing up my roof from his van and I wait for him to walk up the drive to push the doorbell. Oh, no, THE DOORBELL!

And, too late, what credibility I had pieced together cringes at the anticipation of the Batman themed doorbell ring, which until that morning had seemed an appropriate ice breaker.

What all the commotion was about

There once was a man with a heart who lived and laughed with a woman of smiles. They were loud and happy.

The woman of smiles was especially happy, more than she had been in her whole smiley life. And the man's heart was beating louder and was growing bigger than it had in his whole life. This was because of a new life growing and smiling inside the woman.

In the year when Fear was noisier than usual, when hearts beat softer and smiles were smaller, the world began to quieten. So the man and the woman took their loud and happy life and the new life that was growing and smiling and went out into the Fear to make some fresh Commotion.

The man with the heart and the woman of smiles were very good at Commotion. They had both been good at this many years before they met, and once they came together the Commotion just grew and grew. They really couldn't help themselves.

One day, after an especially loud day, the man with the heart and the woman of smiles found a house that needed a fresh heart and they stopped to talk.

They asked the house about its story and found the more they talked, the more they liked the house. The house found that they more they listened, the louder its heart was beating and very soon its heart was beating in time with the man's heart and it began to reflect the woman's smiles.

The woman became smilier and smilier the more they talked and the man's heart beat stronger and stronger the more they talked and soon the Commotion began.

As the Commotion grew, the noisy Fear became annoyed and walked off in a huff. And as the Fear faded into the distance, the other houses began to look up and heard the new Commotion.

The more they listened the more they wanted to join in.

Now the thing about Commotion is that once it starts it is very difficult to stop. The man with the heart and the woman of smiles knew this from years of practice and so it was no surprise to them when the whole street began to shake with loud heart beats and smiley laughters.

The man with the heart and the woman of smiles soon made their home of Commotion with the house and the street became the noisiest street it had ever been. And in the middle of the Commotion the new life, who was growing inside the woman of smiles, laughed out loud into her arms.

Right at that moment of highest Commotion, the man felt his heart beat the loudest it had ever beat and the woman felt the biggest smile that she had ever smiled grow onto her face.

And that was just the start of what all the Commotion was about.

The Purple People

The Redeemer Purple People come in many sizes, from small to extra-large – some are quiet and smiley, while others are louder and chatty. What they have in common, apart from the obvious distinctive pigment, is a welcoming demeanour that makes you feel that you have perhaps met them before or that you would like to meet them again.

I first met a Purple Person as I climbed the steps, looking for reassurance that I wasn't late and that I wouldn't stand out too much in my nervous newness. I'm not sure what it was about their purpleness, but I felt one step closer to acceptance as I walked into the warm.

I saw the matching purple banners and smiled at the attention to detail and the attention given to me which, while practiced, was far from forced and held a genuine purpleness.

I met other Purple People at intervals, each with the purple family likeness of a smile, even though their heritage varied in shade. The further I walked, the more I relaxed and found that some of the Purple People weren't wearing the signature purple tee shirts, but it was clear they came from the same palette because their welcome carried the same purple weight and the same authentic purpleness.

This shouldn't have been surprising, as I soon discovered that they each bore the same purple family likeness of the Purple King who welcomes everyone.

[Explainer: At church the Welcome team wear purple tee shirts. The church's website and banners also are predominantly purple.]

The Red Folk

The Red-Folk are well known to some, but less well known to others. You see, the Red-Folk do their reddy-ness in the background with the smallest folk. This means that bigger folk will only notice them if they have small folk friends.

The Red-Folk are quite distinct; I don't mean their tomato redness, I mean their ability to fold themselves small.

Now, you may know that small folk are very used to legs and knees and big feet and are they are very, very good at winding their way through a forest of trousers and skirts to get to where they need to go. But this can be tiring, and sometimes small folk misjudge the sway of a leg or a knee and bounce off them, falling back onto their bottoms. This can sometimes be funny, but it is often painful and can spark small folk tears.

So, when small folk find that the Red-Folk just love to fold their legs and knees away and come down to small folk level, you can imagine the sheer joy the small folk feel.

Some Red-Folk don't last long because their legs and knees begin to ache, and the small folk noise becomes too loud and the Red-Folk miss 'Big Conversation.' But there are some Red-Folk who are excellent at folding their legs and knees away and who love nothing better than small conversations with small folk. You see they have discovered that this is where small and precious truths are first planted to later become stronger big truths and they have seen that this is also where small folk plant big love in the Red-Folk's big hearts.

So, if you are looking for the Red-Folk, you need to look down to where the small important conversations are taking place with the small important folk.

[Explainer: At church the adults who work with children wear red tee shirts.]

The Trees of Richmond Park

Within a few years of it being established, the Tree Keepers decided to lock Richmond Park between dusk and dawn - for the Trees of Richmond Park were known to hunt at night.

By day they sunned themselves and smiled, and seemed content with their well rooted existence. But they hunted at night.

So, although hemmed in and tagged by curious men, after sundown the Trees of Richmond Park hunted freely in packs within the Park's walls. Oak was the largest tribe (slow but relentless), then Beech (clever in coordinated assaults) with hangers on: Hawthorn (quick on flat ground), Blackthorn (vicious in attack), Birch (a graceful, brutal warrior), and Hornbeam (clumsy, but tolerated for their tough temperament).

The Trees of Richmond Park prided themselves on their stealth; slothful in appearance, apparently careless of the game around them. But they hunted at night.

They granted a place for the birds to nest, yes, that's true, they lulled them into a false sense of safe space and even allowed them to nurture their young. This replenished their stock, their lively larder, but - they hunted at night.

The slower, tastier, ground nesting birds were the easiest prey - the grey partridge, the reed bunting, stonechat and meadow pipit all succumbed - their brittle bones breaking easily against a well-placed low swing of a gnarly bough.

The swifter raptors repeatedly evaded the hunt and gloried in their survival and so the Trees of Richmond Park grew to tolerate their lack of veneration. Not so for the rabbits and squirrels of Bone Copse who were far too foolish to grasp the danger they danced with and they assumed too late that their burrow-nests were impervious to a delving nocturn root, to a dawning yawning crevice - to population cull.

There was talk of young deer disappearing within the Queen's Saw Pit Plantation, but nothing was ever proven. Rumour also had it that the Trees were responsible for an occasional missing child down in Gibbet Wood where a bad-tempered Blackthorn resided. That was hushed up and the parents were persuaded by the generous Crown compensation scheme which had been established and maintained for these and similar incidents.

However, it remained true (at least in the main) that the Trees of Richmond Park hunted at night.

It was in the dark that they pinned their prey. It was in the damp dark that they sucked their fill and nurtured their own, silently, stealthily filling every branch with their hungry young. And they regularly sent their emissaries to claim yet more of the dark with scant regard for the territories claimed or boundaries drawn by come-lately day creatures. And so they established outposts outside the curfewed walls, securing first rights on any and all nutrients further abroad.

Yes, the Trees of Richmond Park chiefly hunted at night and, as apex predator, they have gone unchallenged. They have out-hunted, out-delved, out-witted, out-seeded, out-lived all contenders and they still occupy their dead of hunted night.

But, Billy, they are still known to take the occasional child to feed their young. And that is why it was not a good idea to uproot that sapling.

Stay close, and let's get back to the car.

Deborah's Daughter

The following is an extended sample from the novella, Deborah's Daughter, by Steve Page, published under the name, S J Page.

PROLOGUE
MONDAY MORNING

The words on the cubicle wall bothered me more than they should have done – at least that was my first thought. Sitting there, I couldn't help but feel, against all logic, that they were directed at me and last night's drama, or at least poking fun at it.

I focused on the task at hand as much as I could, but my eyes were drawn back to the red ink adjacent to my right cheek, fresher than the others and closer to the truth.

Were they the same words she said or just similar? Was someone using her dialogue? Or were they simply using the same source material?

'And so, are you resolved to be my

travelling companion this morning?'

The message stood out – partly because graffiti wasn't a big problem here (Mrs. Braddle, the head caretaker, was usually quick to stamp down on it) and partly because of the meticulous nature of the script. Mum might even recognise the marks of a fellow professional: the letters' spacing was uniform, which, compared to the more typical scribbles, was unusual. It must have taken some concentration, probably some steady squatting facing the wall. I could not imagine anyone sitting and twisting at an angle that allowed them to achieve this. How did they sit and to write that perfectly? – maybe a leftie would have found it easier, but even then, I doubted it. The font size was so even, almost as if they had been stencilled. Ha – that was it, not a feat of penmanship after all.

But that still left the message itself, the question, maybe an offer – apparently aimed at me and definitely fresh. It wasn't there on Friday. Could it have been put there as a follow-up to Sunday night's madness? I wasn't sure how, but the evidence was staring me in the face. I finished and stood to sort my clothing.

'What the..!'

I said it out loud, such was my surprise. At eye level was a follow-up message – same ink, same penmanship or stencil-ship. This time not asking a question, but instead giving a response – though an ambiguous one. And the echo from last night was unmistakable.

'And at night you urge me, with great mystery,

to start before the ladies are stirring ...'

I felt a chill and realised that I had been standing there, belt still not fastened, for a while, silently absorbing the message. Was it meant as an encouragement, a reinforcement of the night before? I wasn't sure, but it felt like a simple reminder of my confusion and uncertainty – and for some reason I started crying. I guess the previous night's encounter had upset me more than I'd realised.

I pulled a wodge of toilet paper and wiped my face and blew my nose – too loudly it seemed: "Mo, you alright in there?" Tess's voice came through the door.

"Yeah – just something I ate I think, you go ahead."

I put myself together, got out my phone and captured both messages, so they could haunt me later. ...

...

I was last to get to English. And I didn't recognise the teacher who stared down on us – he was freakishly tall and old – like he should have retired years ago. He was what I imagined a crime fighter brought out of retirement would look like – trying a little too hard, weathered and reluctant, but not out of shape – not to be messed with. I thought that I could also read a hint of uncertainty in his face, like he felt a little out of place. Like he'd been sucked into an alternate reality where the planet's tilt seemed a little off to him.

He didn't say a word, just stood there while we found our desks and once we were quiet, he spoke – really softly but with a deep, don't-mess-with-me, voice, just as expected.

"Good Monday morning, class. My name is Mr. Oke, and I'll be standing in for Mr. Hatchard for the remainder of the Spring term." He cleared his throat, as if trying to get an old instrument back into working order. "I'm looking forward to getting to know each of you at the term progresses. I know you've been working on your set texts since the start of January. I see from Mr. Hatchard's notes that you're working on something called the…" He paused to look at his notes. "…Sisterhood of the Travelling Pants." By the look on his face, he couldn't quite believe what he was reading. "Whilst I'm sure that this novel has much to offer, we'll be pausing your exploration of that saga for the remainder of this term." The class stirred suspiciously at that. He had our full attention.

"Next week we will start Brighton Rock by Graham Greene. However - " Oke paused as the class erupted with protest.

"But sir, we're already reading Sisterhood -

"What? But we're part way through and started our –

"But why, sir – that's not fair!"

"However - " Oke had to raise his voice above the din.

"HOWEVER – please calm down and let me finish."

Now it was me who felt like I had just been sucked into an alternative timeline – a 'What If?' experiment. I think he could see that just maybe he'd started off on the wrong foot but was committed now.

The murmurs of protest subsided slightly as he continued. "Thank you. As I was saying, however, this coming week we will not be looking at either text. Instead, you will be impressing me with your own writing skills so I can gauge for myself what standard of abilities I am working with here."

I didn't have a great feeling about this at all. They'd switched a fan-favourite for this guy? Hatchard was one of the better teachers – at least he seemed to know what he was doing and we knew where we stood with him. Oke had just turned the whole class against him in his first 5 minutes – he couldn't have done it any more effectively if someone was writing his script. And as I watched him I got the impression he wondered if he'd taken things a little too far.

"Listen to my instructions carefully and then I'll take three questions. He switched the interactive board on and ten phrases appeared.

Oh, no.

'I've lifted several of the less colourful missives from the toilet walls this morning. Here they are in all their glory ..."

I didn't hear his next words – I was transfixed by the two messages that sat in my photos, reproduced here for all to see amongst the others. I looked around, no one seemed shocked, just amused, or in Tess's case, perplexed.

"... Any questions?" Oke had stopped talking and looked expectantly at the class. As he answered the thin diet of questions from some of my bolder classmates,

I pieced together what he wanted. We were to use these as a trigger for a short story.

"You can choose any one of these – as a first line or a title or simply as a theme to weave into your story."

He proceeded to read the lines one by one.

- I wish I was back in Kefalonia
- Let me out of here
- I don't understand the question, but the answer is 8
- A person who has never made a mistake, has never tried algebra
- And so, are you resolved to be my travelling companion this morning?
- It's chocolate pizza again
- When will this end?
- And at night you urge me, with great mystery, to start before the ladies are stirring ...
- Education is the most powerful weapon, but I'm out of bullets
- One fun fact is one too many

"There should be enough choice there for you.

Take your rulers and draw a line down the centre of your page." This was getting more bizarre by the minute; it was nothing like our normal English lesson.

The more he talked, the less 'don't mess with me' he seemed and the more passionate he sounded. His enthusiasm for the exercise looked genuine - at least that made one of us.

"On each page only write on the left-hand side – this is essential. And do not try to perfect your style or grammar – just get the words down no matter how inadequate they seem. What's important is the sound of activity, the murmur of pens engaged with paper. I will talk you through the process of redrafting and making use of that empty space on the right in the days to come. Today just write. Begin."

He cut off the rumble of dissent with a shake of his head and a practiced smile and gradually we each bowed to the inevitable. Apparently, he was serious; he sat at his desk and got out an expensive looking leather notebook and started writing himself.

After a pause, I suppressed the prickly heat of distrust and took a breath. Maybe this was good. Like an explanatory flash-back scene capturing what happened might help me make sense of it; I started writing, taking myself back to last night, to when I first heard those antiquated phrases:

Sunday Night

I opened my eyes at five past midnight not sure what had woken me up. I turned over, away from the glow of the clock, and found myself staring into a pale face. It spoke in a cold whisper: "*Deborah...*".

CHAPTER I
SUNDAY NIGHT

In which curiosity is woken
and sleep is denied

Sunday night

I opened my eyes at five past midnight, not sure what had woken me up. I turned over, away from the glow of the clock and found myself staring into a pale face. It spoke in a cold whisper: "*Deborah...*".

"Gran? – what are you doing up?"

She smiled – with an unfamiliar mischievous look in her eyes - '*And, so, are you resolved to be my travelling companion? I urge you to start before the ladies are stirring...*'

"Wha..?"

"*Come, child – clothe yourself and come.*"

She turned, paused to take a book from my shelf and then shuffled off and out into the hall towards her room. By the time I caught up with her she was peering into a small brown case which was usually poking out from under her bed. She was placing the book inside; I looked over her shoulder and saw a curious collection which I recognised from around the house - a radiator key, a coaster, a tea strainer.

As she noticed me, she moved her shoulder to screen the contents a little more, slowly closed the lid and then stopped still, like a child hoping they wouldn't be noticed.

"Gran?"

She turned and gave me that cheeky smile again.

"*Not yet*", she said, "*that will be coming later. Retrieve the Commodore, pet.*"

These were the most words she'd strung together in months. It was wonderful to hear, but part of me dreaded returning to those frenetic times. I sighed. "Come on Gran, let's get you back to bed."

She raised herself to her full height and glared - all mischief covered by a snarl. Oh no. " - *get the Commodore Pet, you wicked child!*"

I hadn't seen her like this for a while. Gone was the placid, patient grandmother, replaced by the belligerent child of a woman that she had been before the new medicine had kicked in.

I softened my voice, "Of course gran, show me."
"*Stupid, child – here.*" She moved slowly but purposely to her wardrobe. "*Here.*" She removed a pile of loose balls of wool which I recognised from a lifetime ago, and uncovered a cute looking, toy-like, desk top computer – a 'Commodore PET 200' according to the front badge. A tiny, curved monitor sat on a keyboard – it looked like someone's imagined home computer back when they were just science fiction. I wasn't sure what she wanted me to do with this – but I hoped she wasn't expecting it to work. I tried not to be phased, but Gran saw me hesitate and slapped me hard, "*Don't slack. Do - as - you - are - told.*" Then she seemed to lose her thread and rubbed my arm – "*I'm sorry, oh, I'm sorry. It's not right. I can't do it. You'll have to.*" She sat at the dressing table and slumped, "*Please, child.*"
I shuddered. Mum and I had seen Gran's personality slowly fade and be replaced by a new angry character and then, as the medication took hold, she'd become this spent, benign and docile husk of the radiant woman I had grown up with. What was going on now?

I think it was how pathetic she looked and the plea in her voice that decided it for me – I reached in and lifted the Commodore onto her table and tried to figure out how to plug it in. It was nothing like the desktops at school – it was smaller, like a toy. I think some part of Gran's brain could see I needed help and took over with tuts and sighs, her trembling hands finding the right socket and somehow between us we attached the cable and plugged it in. I watched and could see how much effort it took her, but her body relaxed a little as she found the power switch, and we watched the screen emerge from the black into a dull green. Conscious of the beeps it was making, I closed her door and together we watched the screen slowly come alive with green text on a grey-green background. And then, once it stopped its start-up routine, it was as if it had thrown a switch in Gran's head – she sat straighter, pushed her shoulders back and began typing. The movement reminded me of a secretary in a scene from some old movie; the whole thing looked comical, but I caught a glimpse of the woman she had been before dementia stole her from us.

I couldn't follow the words on the tiny screen, but I sat and watched her – hoping she'd get whatever this was out of her system. I'm not sure how long we were there or how often I dozed, but after a while something in her movements made me start and I looked up to see her poised but still. She looked at me with a satisfied look on her face and simply said "Printer." I went back to the wardrobe and there on the floor was a printer – matching the Commodore in size and style. I rummaged and found some cables and after a lot of trial and error, figured out the connections. Gran waited and then nodded, hit a few command keys and her text slowly printed onto greyed A4 paper. I waited and after an age the printer stilled and pushed a neatly typed document onto the tray. The whole exercise seemed to have drained Gran and before the last page had finished she had shuffled back to her bed. *"Make sure you leave nothing of our venture. You have your task. We'll speak again come night fall."*

Confused and tired, I packed the Commodore and printer away and went back to my room carrying the pages with care.

Some instinct suggested that this wasn't something to leave lying around, and I went to put it in my school bag. The last line caught my eye – 'Deborah Jael Mortz, of the Order of the Daughters of Deborah.' My curiosity beat my tiredness and I started to read from the beginning. The more I read, the more confused I was. Was this real? Or was Gran just delusional? I went to bed, overwhelmed with questions - but one dominated the others as I drifted off: Who were these Daughters of Deborah?

If you enjoyed this taster of you can continue Mo's story in the novella, *Deborah's Daughter* by S J Page, available where you got this collection.

Acknowledgements

There are many who have assisted me to get to the stage of compiling my writing in this way. I must give a bit shout out to Arvon Foundation, a charity that runs writing course, events and retreats – you can find their resources online. Equally, thank you to the Poetry School who started me on this journey, again you can find them online.

Closer to home thank you to Pete Cornford, my pastor at Redeemer London [www.redeemerlondon.org] who enthused me to put my first collection together. And I must express my admiration and thanks to Sam Isaacson (look up his books at http://thealtimer.wordpress.com) who has given me much need advice over the past few years.

And thank you to you for picking up this collection. I encourage you to go into a bar, order a soda and lime and strike up a conversation. Or maybe sit in a corner with a note pad and people watch for a while. You'll see plenty of stories to be told.

Also from Steve Page

If you enjoyed this collection, you just might enjoy

Not Too Big To Weep;

Not Too Old To Dance;

Not Too Soon For Christmas;

Wisdom Poetry;

Fruity Poetry; and

Father is a Verb.

If you still want more, you can find me amongst a world-wide crowd of poets on https://hellopoetry.com

Til next time -